DREAMWORKS

DRAGONS

UNDER THE DRAGON'S SPELL

igloobooks

igl+books

Published in 2016
by Igloo Books Ltd
Cottage Farm
Sywell
NN6 0BJ
www.igloobooks.com

Designed by Matt Hamilton
Edited by Gemma Rose

HUN001 0816
2 4 6 8 10 9 7 5 3 1
ISBN: 978-1-78557-418-4

Printed and manufactured in China

Hiccup had called all the Dragon Riders to his house for a special meeting.
He had something important to show them. When everyone
was seated, Hiccup turned to Toothless and said, "Go ahead, bud."
Toothless lit up Hiccup's room and, through the Dragon Eye, a projection
appeared on the wall. The Dragon Riders all gasped.

"There are areas and symbols here I've never seen before," Fishlegs said. He turned to look at Hiccup. "You realise this map..."

"... goes beyond the boundaries of the archipelago," Hiccup finished his sentence for him. "I know."

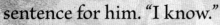

The group was quiet for a moment. Astrid broke the silence. "So what's our next move?" she asked.

The next morning, Hiccup presented the map to the Viking leaders. Spitelout was the first one to give his opinion. "I think you all know as well as I do that when you go looking for trouble, you usually find it."

"I'm with Spitelout," Sven said. "If that Dragon Eye leads to unknown places and new dragons, then no good will come from any of that."

Stoick spoke to the Viking leaders next. "Nothing is more important than peace. Think of the most important thing in the world to you. How far would you be willing to go to get it?" Stoick looked at Hiccup. "This boy's whole life has been dragons. We couldn't stop him if we wanted to, so we might as well support him."

Hiccup and Toothless started to leave. Stoick turned to Toothless. "You take care of my boy, dragon," he said, and Toothless nodded.

The next day at dawn, all the Dragon Riders set out to explore the new territory they saw on the map. "Into the great beyond!" the riders cheered.

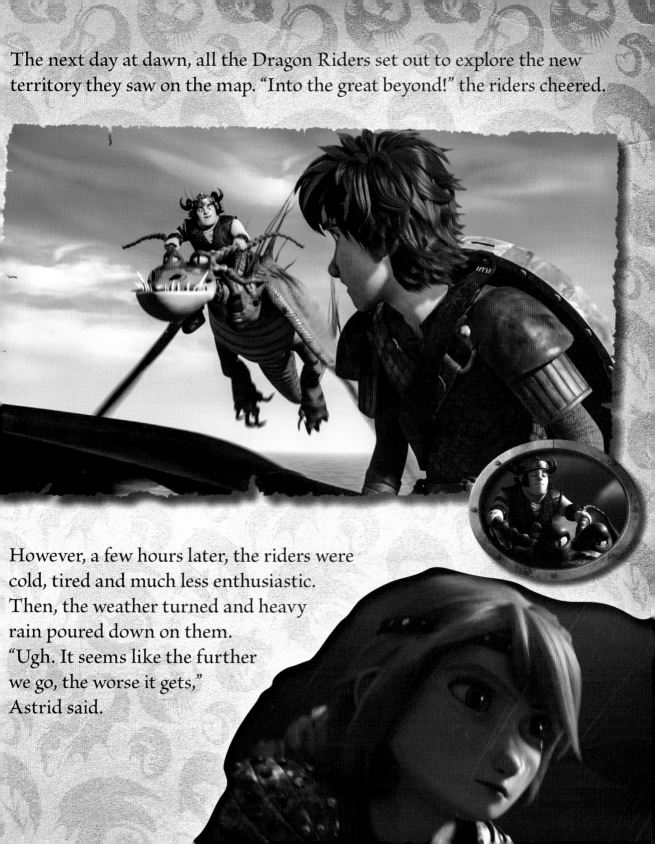

However, a few hours later, the riders were cold, tired and much less enthusiastic. Then, the weather turned and heavy rain poured down on them. "Ugh. It seems like the further we go, the worse it gets," Astrid said.

Suddenly, Hiccup spotted a patch of light ahead.
"Everybody, fly to the light," he instructed.
The riders broke through the rough weather and into sunshine.
Directly below them was a landscape of new islands.

"We made it, Hiccup!"
Astrid cheered. "We made it!"
Hiccup pointed out a place where they
could land, but the dragons had other
ideas. The dragons all pulled their riders
towards a different island.
"What is it, girl?" Fishlegs asked his dragon.
"Don't you want to rest?"

As they landed, the riders heard a strange musical sound coming from the island. It was the most beautiful place they had ever seen, with gorgeous beaches and fruit trees everywhere.

"Okay, I'm never going back to Berk," Snotlout announced.
Hiccup grinned. "I guess we all agree on where we're camping out for the night."

"Great!" Snotlout said. "I'll take care of the fire." He pulled out a jar and poured a trail of gel on the ground. "Hookfang, light it up!" he ordered. Soon, there was a warm fire.

"Monstrous Nightmare gel. Don't leave home without it," Snotlout said.

"Um, that looks dangerous," Hiccup said. He took the jar away from Snotlout for safekeeping. Before long, all the dragons and their riders fell into a blissful sleep, lulled by the strange music.

The next morning,
Hiccup woke up to
silence. He walked over
to Astrid and shook her
awake. "Astrid, wake up.
Do you hear that?"
Astrid opened her eyes
sleepily and listened.
"What? I don't hear anything," she said.
"Exactly," Hiccup said. "That sound is gone."

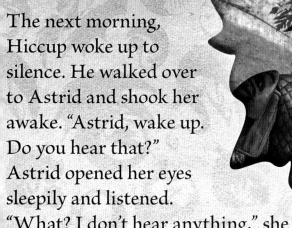

All of a sudden, Fishlegs appeared at Hiccup's side.
"So are our dragons," Fishlegs told him. "All of them. Gone!"

The Dragon Riders looked around the island for their missing dragons, when suddenly, Toothless appeared. He pounced on Hiccup, knocking him to the ground. Then, he raced around the camp, roaring.

Snotlout turned to Hiccup. "I think your dragon ate something weird, because he's out of his mind."

Fishlegs disagreed. "I think he's trying to tell us something."

Hiccup jumped on Toothless. "You guys stay here in case the rest of the dragons come back. Toothless and I are going to look for them from above."

As Hiccup and Toothless searched the sky, Hiccup
noticed something below. A Thunderdrum dragon
was heading straight towards the defenceless
Dragon Riders.

Then, the mysterious music began again. Toothless tried to fly in
the direction of the music, but Hiccup convinced him to steer the
Thunderdrum away from the riders and deeper into the forest.
"We need to find our dragons now," Hiccup said to the riders.
"We'll all go together."

As the group walked on, the beautiful island turned dark. They discovered a boneyard of dragon skeletons and broken pieces of amber-coloured rock. Then, they heard a distressed screech in the distance. "What was that?" Snotlout asked.

"That, my friends, is a dragon in trouble," Fishlegs told them. They raced towards the troubling sound and discovered a group of dragons all encased in amber.

From out of nowhere the music began again, even louder than before.
A huge, strange-looking dragon landed on a rock and roared.
It looked like a new species.
Toothless and all the riders huddled out of sight as it picked up one of the amber rocks and flew off with it. Toothless immediately tried to follow the dragon's song. "No, Toothless! No, bud!" Hiccup yelled and pulled hard on his reins. Reluctantly, Toothless stopped. Hiccup turned to the group. "It's the song. It draws the dragons in."

"We need to call that dragon something," Fishlegs said.

"I'm thinking Deathsong," replied Tuffnut. "You know, because if you hear the song, you're probably dead soon."

"He's got a point," said Hiccup.

It didn't take long for the riders to find their dragons trapped in the amber rock. Before the Dragon Riders could help, the Deathsong sprayed them with the amber.

Soon, everyone but Hiccup and Astrid was trapped. Hiccup was trying to help Toothless when Astrid cried out, "Hiccup, it's coming for you!" As the Deathsong came closer, Astrid pushed Hiccup out of the way and she got sprayed instead. Hiccup fell down a ravine, only to find himself face-to-face with the Thunderdrum dragon.

"Oh, hey, remember me?" Hiccup joked. The dragon roared.

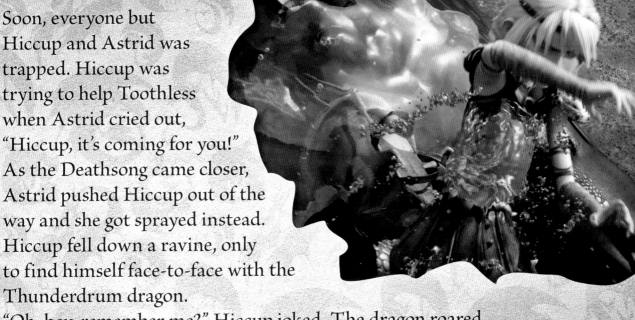

Before Hiccup could react, the Deathsong soared back into view and prepared to take on the Thunderdrum. Hiccup shot a bolo from his shield and the thick cord wrapped around the Deathsong's snout. "That won't hold him for long," Hiccup told the Thunderdrum. "You're not going to like what I do next, but trust me, this is going to work out for the best for both of us." Then, he jumped on the Thunderdrum's back and flew off just as the Deathsong broke free of the bolo.

The Thunderdrum flew wildly, trying to throw Hiccup off his back. "I'm trying to help," Hiccup said to the dragon. "Don't you listen?" Then, he remembered Thunderdrums were hard of hearing. Hiccup stared at the mighty dragon. "That means you can't be lured by the Deathsong's call. You know what, Mr. Thunderdrum? You're going to help me get my friends back."

The Thunderdrum seemed to understand and let Hiccup pet him.

Hiccup and the Thunderdrum returned to the riders. At first they tried to break open the amber rocks by having the Thunderdrum slam into them, but it was no use.

"Forget it, Hiccup," Fishlegs said from inside the amber. "Once this stuff cools down, it's as hard as any rock I've ever seen."

"Cools down," Hiccup repeated to himself, thinking hard.

Hiccup leapt off the Thunderdrum, took out Snotlout's jar of Monstrous Nightmare gel and spread it around each dragon and rider. Just then the Deathsong returned, ready to fight the Thunderdrum.

As the two dragons rushed at each other to fight, Hiccup struck his shield on the ground, creating a massive spark. Fire raced along the trail of gel, melting all the amber. The dragons were freed first and quickly plucked their riders away from the melting rocks.

"Snotlout! You watch the Thunderdrum, I'll take care of the Deathsong," Hiccup yelled. Hiccup and Toothless fired away at the Deathsong, slowly drawing it away from the Thunderdrum. They led the Deathsong on a chase across the island.

"Let's relocate this guy permanently," said Hiccup. He spotted a cave opening ahead and they flew inside, the Deathsong in hot pursuit. "Now get us out of here, bud," Hiccup told Toothless. Toothless used his echolocation to find another way out of the cave. They raced out, with the Deathsong right behind them. Toothless unleashed a sonic blast at the cave opening, causing a rock collapse and trapping the Deathsong inside.

"Nice going," Hiccup said. "Nobody's going to hear his song in there."
The island was quiet; no one would be lured by the Deathsong's music again.
Hiccup met up with his friends and the Thunderdrum, who now realised the riders meant him no harm. "Guys, I want to apologise," he told his friends, as they headed off to explore more of the new territory. "I'm sorry for getting you into this. If you want to turn back..."
"Are you kidding?" Astrid said.
"This is the most fun we've had in years," Snotlout agreed.

"There is one thing," Astrid said. "We need our own island."

"I agree. We need a base of operations," Hiccup said. He turned to Snotlout. "You're the man of the hour. You brought the Monstrous Nightmare gel. You get to choose where we go next."

Snotlout beamed and pointed into the distance.

"To the great beyond!" he shouted.

"To the great beyond!" all the riders cheered as they flew off to their next adventure.